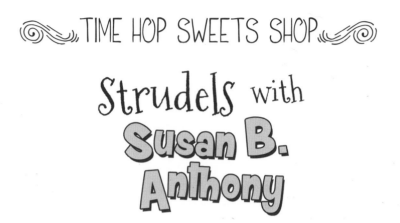

TIME HOP SWEETS SHOP

Strudels with Susan B. Anthony

By Kyla Steinkraus

Illustrated by Katie Wood

D0104641

Rourke
Educational Media
rourkeeducationalmedia.com

www.rourkeeducationalmedia.com

Edited by: Keli Sipperley
Cover and Interior layout by: Kathy Walsh
Cover and Interior Illustrations by: Katie Wood

Library of Congress PCN Data

Strudels with Susan B. Anthony / Kyla Steinkraus
 (Time Hop Sweet Shops)
 ISBN 978-1-68342-332-4 (hard cover)(alk. paper)
 ISBN 978-1-68342-428-4 (soft cover)
 ISBN 978-1-68342-498-7 (e-Book)
 Library of Congress Control Number: 2017931178

Printed in the United States of America,
North Mankato, Minnesota

Dear Parents and Teachers,

Fiona and Finley are just like any modern-day kids. They help out with the family business, face struggles and triumphs at school, travel through time with important historical figures …

Well, maybe that part's not so ordinary. At the Time Hop Sweets Shop, anything can happen, at any point in time. The family bakery draws customers from all over the map—and all over the history books. And when Tick Tock the parrot squawks, Fiona and Finley know an adventure is about to begin!

These beginner chapter books are designed to introduce students to important people in U.S. history, turning their accomplishments into adventures that Fiona, Finley, and young readers get to experience right along with them.

Perfect as read-alouds, read-alongs, or independent readers, books in the Time Hop Sweets Shop series were written to delight, inform, and engage your child or students by making each historical figure memorable and relatable. Each book includes a biography, comprehension questions, websites for further reading, and more.

We look forward to our time travels together!

Happy Reading,
Rourke Educational Media

Table of Contents

One Vote for Strudels

"Taste this," Finley said to his little sister, Fiona. He held up an apple strudel with lots of frosting. "It's yummy!"

Fiona shook her head. She helped Dad mix cookie dough in a bowl. "I'm not hungry."

Their parents owned the Sweets Shop. It was a bakery with old-fashioned treats like Washington cake and green tomato pie. Finley and Fiona helped make desserts after school.

"Why not?" Finley asked.

"I'm too busy thinking about the vote." Fiona was running for school president. "If we give away cookies, do you think people will vote for me? When I'm president, we'll have ice cream for lunch every day."

"Hmm," Dad said "I'm not sure that's the best use of power."

The bell over the door jingled. "Look at the time!" their pet parrot, Tick Tock, squawked. "Look at the time!"

A woman with dark hair and a long dress walked in. "Did I hear someone say 'vote'? I

smell fresh apple strudel! My favorite!"

Fiona put a piece of strudel on a plate. She handed it to the woman. "You're in the right place! I'm trying to get people to vote for me."

The woman smiled. "How wonderful. In my day, women couldn't vote at all."

Finley's face lit up. "Are you Susan B. Anthony?"

Susan took a bite of strudel. "Yes, I am. When I was in school, I wanted to learn long division. My teacher told me girls didn't need to learn things like long division."

"Girls can learn math just like boys!" Fiona said. She nudged Finley. "In fact, some girls are better."

"Hey!" Finley yelped.

"Girls and boys can be great at anything."

Susan said. "But in my time, women don't have the right to live and work like they want to. Women aren't allowed to vote. Married women can't own land. Girls can't go to college."

"Wowza!" Fiona yelled. "I can't believe it!"

"No yelling," Finley said. His sister was always loud. He turned down his hearing aid.

"Luckily, things can change. Would you like to come on a trip with me?"

Now it was Finley's turn to yell. "Yes!"

"Let's go to Rochester, New York," Susan said, her eyes sparkling. "It is November 5th, 1872, the day of the presidential election."

Fiona and Finley waved goodbye to Dad. They raced to the side door. "See you soon!"

Tick Tock cawed. The Sweets Shop shook and spun and whirled.

Fighting for Freedom

Finley and Fiona landed in a heap. Finley groaned. Fiona jumped to her feet. She was wearing a long black dress, just like Susan. Finley wore an old-fashioned suit.

A few men in the same type of suits sat around a large box. They wrote on ballots and dropped them in the box. They were voting. Two large posters hung on the wall behind the table with the ballot box. One poster said "Vote for Ulysses S. Grant." The other poster said "Vote for Horace Greeley."

Susan B. Anthony stood up straight, smoothing her black dress with her hands. She walked up to the table. Fiona and Finley followed her. "Please give me a ballot."

The men stared at her. They didn't say anything.

She looked them in the eyes. "I am a citizen of the United States. I have the

right to vote." She pulled out a paper and put it on the table. "This is the Fourteenth Amendment of the Constitution. It says citizens can vote."

One of the men shook his head. "Only male citizens have the right to vote."

"Failure is impossible! I must vote."

The man sighed. "I'm not going to stop you."

"Really?" Susan B. Anthony's eyes widened. She filled in her ballot and put her vote in the ballot box. "Now I've gone and done it," she said with a smile.

"What now?" Finley asked. "You voted, but it's illegal."

"Let's go back to my house," Susan said. "We can have tea and talk. Ready?"

Changing the World

The room whirled and spun. Finley groaned and held his head. They were in Susan B. Anthony's parlor, a very fancy room. Finley sat on the edge of a fancy couch.

Susan handed them each a fancy cup of tea. "Drink up!"

"What happened after you voted?" Fiona asked worriedly.

"A police officer came to my house and arrested me. They put me in handcuffs. At my trial, the judge told the jury to find me guilty. I said, 'I will never pay a dollar of your unjust penalty'."

"That's so unfair!" Fiona said.

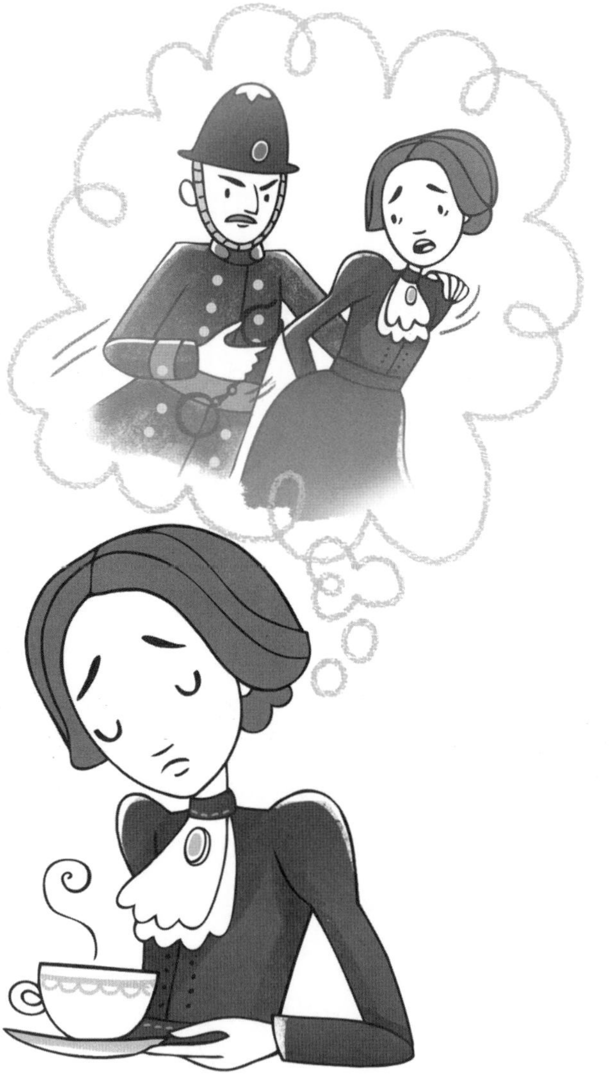

"I didn't let anything stop me," Susan said with a laugh. "After that, I did everything I could to spread the word. I traveled alone by train or carriage. I even braved snowstorms in open sleighs. I talked about suffrage—women's right to vote. We needed to change the laws that hurt women. I urged women to stand up for themselves. It wasn't always easy. People booed and hissed. They threw tomatoes and rotten eggs at me."

"That's horrible," Finley said.

"Did you ever want to quit?" Fiona asked. She sipped her tea. It was delicious.

"Working to change the way people think is hard," Susan said. "We must be strong!"

Fiona sighed. "It takes so long to change things!"

"That's true. But change does happen.

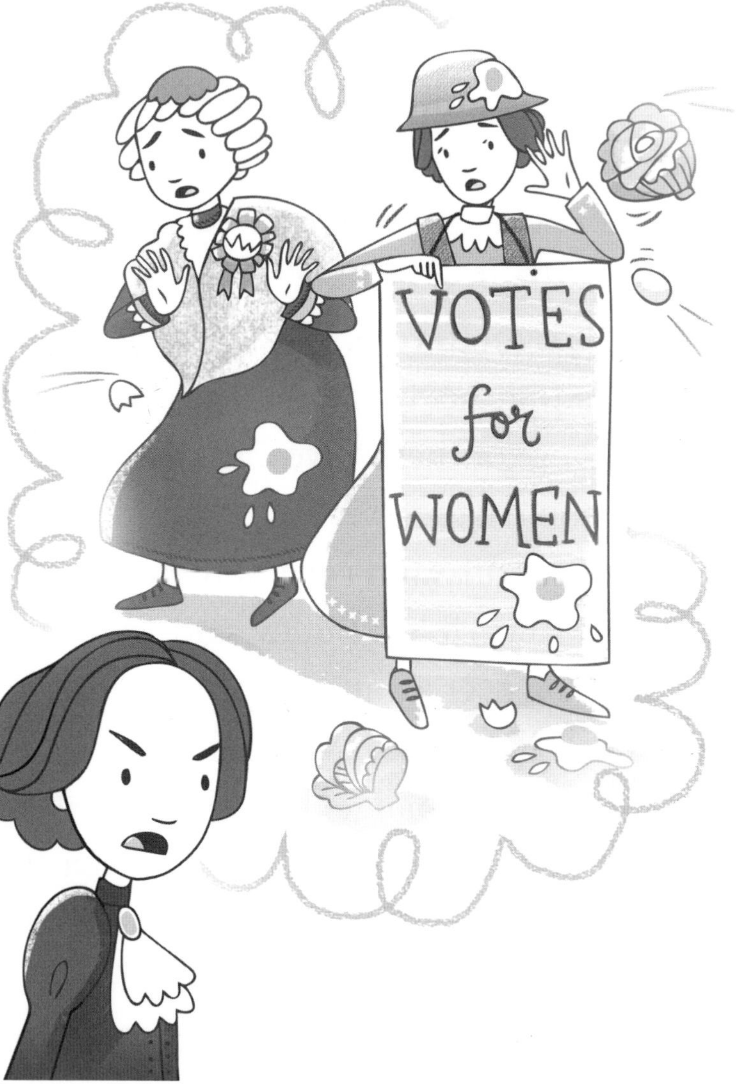
VOTES
for
WOMEN

In 1860, we won a huge victory. In New York, women won the right to own their own property. They could have a business in their own name. I spoke in front of Congress every year, urging them to change the law. By 1896, women could vote in Utah, Wyoming, Colorado, and Idaho."

"Wowza!" Fiona said. "You really helped to change things."

"I was once a hated woman, but one day it will seem like everyone loves me," Susan B. Anthony said happily.

"What else did you do?" Finley asked.

"Many things," Susan said. "I made a dear friend named Elizabeth Stanton. We ran a newspaper about women's rights. We published a book about it, too. I said women should be able to wear pants. They should be paid the same as a man for the same work. Elizabeth and I started the National Woman Suffrage Association."

"You did so much," Fiona said. "I'm tired just thinking about it."

"I believed in what I was doing," Susan said. "It was important."

Fiona drank the rest of her tea. "I want to make a difference, too."

"Me too," Finley said.

"Listen to me," Susan said. She patted Fiona's cheek. "Don't worry about other people. Think your best thoughts, speak your best words, work your best works. You will make a difference!"

Finley and Fiona grinned at each other.

"I think it's time you kids went home."

"Thank you!" Fiona said. The kids hugged Susan as the room began to spin.

When they got back to the Sweets Shop, they finished their strudels.

Fiona licked the frosting off her lips. "When I'm president, I'm going to make sure everyone has equal rights."

"I don't think you can do that in first grade," Finley said.

Fiona pumped her fist in the air. "I mean president of the country, silly! Someday, that's going to be me!"

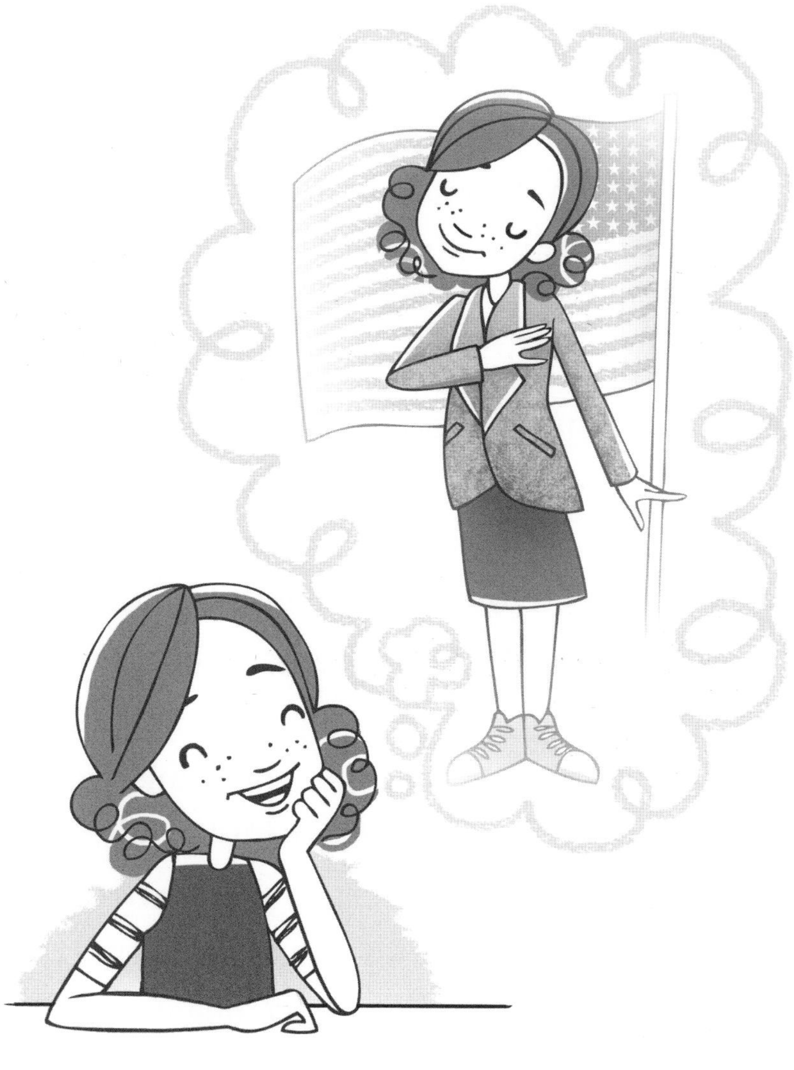

About Susan B. Anthony

Susan B. Anthony was born in 1820 in Adams, Massachusetts. Unlike many people during this time, Susan's father believed girls should get an education. She learned to read when she was four. She loved learning. She went to school and was taught at home. When Susan was a teenager, she became a teacher. She chose not to marry, because she didn't want to give up her freedom. Susan and her family were part of the Underground Railroad. They helped runaway slaves escape north to Canada, where slavery was illegal.

In 1851, Susan met Elizabeth Cady Stanton, a woman famous for her work with women's rights. The two friends held many meetings on women's suffrage, the right for women to vote. They gave speeches, held meetings, and wrote books and articles. In 1905, Susan met with President Theodore Roosevelt to argue for women's rights. On March 13, 1906, Susan died at the age of 86. After her death, a phrase from her last suffrage speech, "Failure is Impossible," became the motto for people working toward women's voting rights. Fourteen years later, the 19th amendment was passed. It was known as the Susan B. Anthony amendment. In 1920, women finally won the right to vote.

Q and A with Kyla Steinkraus

1) When you start writing, do you already know the ending?

No, I don't! That's one of the best parts of writing. It's as much an adventure for me as the writer as I hope it is for the reader!

2) What impressed you the most about Susan B. Anthony?

She never gave up! She didn't give up when she was arrested. She didn't give up when people booed her or threw things at her. She never gave up, even though it took years and years for things to change.

3) Did you learn anything new in your research?

Susan B. Anthony died before women could vote in every state in the country. However, she was alive when four states made it legal for women to vote. I'm sure she knew it was only a matter of time before all women could vote.

Comprehension Questions

1. What did Susan B. Anthony's teacher tell her?

2. Name three things women couldn't do in Susan B. Anthony's time.

3. Why was Susan B. Anthony arrested?

Websites to Visit

www.ducksters.com/biography/
su/Susan_B._Anthony.php

http://encyclopedia.kids.net.au/page/
su/Susan_B._Anthony

www.softschools.com/facts/biography/
susan_b_anthony_facts/805/

Writing Prompt

Imagine you live in the 1800s, in Susan B. Anthony's time. Would you fight for women's rights? Why or why not? What would you do to help?

About the Author

Kyla Steinkraus lives in Atlanta, Georgia with her husband, two kids, and two spoiled cats. She is the author of more than 30 kids' books. She loves writing and learning about new  things. She is extremely thankful to Susan B. Anthony for fighting for the rights of all women. When she's not writing, Kyla enjoys board games, hiking, reading, and drawing.